Sundblad
800 Lucas Dr.
Sedro Woolley, WA

JAKE O'SHAWNASEY

Written By:
STEPHEN COSGROVE

Illustrated By:
ROBIN JAMES

GROLIER ENTERPRISES INC.
Danbury, Connecticut

A Serendipity Book

Dedicated to the Isle of Ireland, where Jake can always fly free.

S. Cosgrove

The wind blows free in Ireland. It whistles in from the ocean and soars over the Emerald Isle. Birds of all sorts from all over the world flock there to take advantage of the winging winds. There are swallows, eagles, owls and a whole lot of seagulls.

A thousand or more birds sit on the edge of the cliffs that overlook the Atlantic Ocean. They wait for just the right breeze to send them soaring high into the sky with no effort whatsoever.

The seagulls, like the rest of the birds, would constantly take wing just for the fun of flying—all the seagulls, that is, except a strange-looking green Irish seagull by the name of Jake O'Shawnasey.

Now, it wasn't that Jake didn't want to fly. Oh, how he wanted to, but he didn't believe he could fly. And because he didn't believe, he couldn't.

Jake would flap his wings and try desperately to catch a breeze. As he would begin to lift from the ground, flapping his wings furiously, he would think, "I don't think I can fly! In fact . . . I can't!" With that he would fall to the ground with a heavy crash, usually losing eight or ten feathers for his efforts.

Jake O'Shawnasey was not a seagull to give up easily. He tried every trick there was in the Seagull Flying Manual, but nothing would work. Once, out of desperation, Jake grabbed hold of the tail of a kite and soared over one hundred feet into the air. Then, when the kite reached the end of its string, Jake let go.

For a moment it looked as if he might make it. He was flapping his wings magnificently. But then, as always, Jake began thinking he couldn't fly. He stopped flapping his wings. Down he fell, twisting and turning, with feathers floating gently behind him, into the ocean below.

With all his falling and jumping off cliffs, Jake was becoming an absolute menace in the sky. All the birds would constantly look this way and that, in fear of being hit by a falling green seagull.

In desperation, the birds of Ireland held a secret meeting. "We have to do something about Jake!" shouted the swallows. "Sure," croaked the crows, "but what can we do?" They thought and thought.

Finally a wise old owl stepped forward and said, "Possibly I should teach Jake O'Shawnasey The Secret of the Cliffs of County Cort." They stopped and gazed at the cliffs above them. Solemnly, they agreed that The Secret held the only hope of Jake learning to fly. While the other birds cheered him on, the wise old owl flew off to find Jake.

Now, finding Jake had never been a difficult task for any of the birds of Ireland. All they would have to do was look in the water at the base of the cliff and there Jake would be, floundering in the sea. Today was no exception. The wise old owl waited patiently on the beach for Jake to swim ashore. "Jake," said the owl, "do you really want to learn to fly?"

Jake thought for a moment and then answered, "Oh, Yes. I am tired of falling, and I've had five colds already this year from swimming in that cold ocean!"

"What I am about to tell you," said the owl, "is the location of The Secret of the Cliffs of County Cort. With that secret you can learn to fly."

The owl solemnly turned and pointed to the top of the cliff towering above them. "The Secret, Jake, is there at the top. When you find it, you will never have a problem flying again."

Jake took a long look up the cliff. "But how will I get all the way up there?" he asked. "I can barely fly downwards, so how could I possibly fly up?"

"You must do that yourself," said the owl, who flew off to join the other feathered spectators waiting at the top of the cliff.

Jake took a couple of deep breaths of fresh air. He gulped once and began flapping his wings in hopes of flying to the top. His flapping came to a sudden stop when he once again thought, "Oh, I don't believe I can do it!" With that, he fell back with a clunk to the beach below.

"I'll never get to the top by flying because I know I can't fly. But I know how to get to the top without flying." So Jake scurried around, looking for the things that would set his plan in motion.

Jake found a great length of old vine hanging from the rocks. Then he searched the beach until he found an old fishhook. Carefully he lashed it to the end of his vine rope, and finally, with the help of two starfish he strapped to his feet, he was ready to *climb* the cliffs.

Jake carefully threw the fishhook high into the rocks, and when it was secure, he began pulling himself up. With the starfish on his feet he had excellent traction. Step by step he came closer to The Secret of the Cliffs of County Cort.

High above him and all around him he could hear his cheering section urging him upward and onward.

Finally, after many hours of hard climbing, Jake O'Shawnasey reached the top of the Cliffs of County Cort. His friends shouted and cheered as Jake stood there, panting and puffing after his long journey.

"I'm at the top," puffed Jake, "but where is the Secret?" The birds shouted in unison, "It's there, written upon that rock." Jake, for the first time, noticed a large boulder right before him. Carved on the rock was this message:

If you find you're not believing
In everything you do . . .
Just remember lots of trying
Will bring confidence to you.

Jake thought, "I wonder if that could be my problem. Maybe I can fly, if I have confidence in what I'm doing. That's it! I need only to believe in myself and then I can learn to fly!"

Jake carefully unfolded his wings, flapped them once or twice, and found the confidence to bolster his courage. "I know I can do it! I know I can fly! I really and truly believe in myself!"

With that, his wings began to pound, and Jake, as gracefully as any other Irish bird, lifted from the ground and flew high into the sky.

Jake O'Shawnasey was totally confident now. He believed in himself. Because he believed, he could fly!

Jake was so happy, he felt that he could fly without falling for the rest of his life.

So if you're deep in trouble
And don't believe in what you do ...
Just remember Jake O'Shawnasey
And confidence will come to you.

This story would have ended happily, except for one small problem ...

Jake O'Shawnasey never learned how to land.